ISBN 1-59310-402-2

Cover image and interior illustrations by Heather Solum. Design by Steve Bailey.

Published by Barbour Publishing, Inc., P.O. Box 719, Uhrichsville, Ohio 44683, www.barbourbooks.com

Our mission is to publish and distribute inspirational products offering exceptional value and biblical encouragement to the masses.

 Member of the
Evangelical Christian
Publishers Association

Printed in China.
5 4 3 2 1

CHRISTMAS BLESSINGS FOR YOU

DEBORAH BOONE

DayMaker
GREETING BOOKS

CHRISTMAS
IS HERE—

bringing with it all the hustle and bustle of preparation. Malls fill as everyone tries to find the perfect gift for a loved one. Lights are hung and ornaments put on the tree. We find ourselves humming or singing along with all the old familiar carols and pulling out childhood favorites—like Grandma's special oatmeal cookie recipe. The house soon fills with scents of pine boughs and cinnamon and gaily wrapped packages with beautifully tied ribbon. And best of all, good friends and family are coming in the door. As we celebrate anew the Savior's birth, I wish for you all the heart-warming memories and blessings Christmas may bestow.

GELEBRATE THE SEASON

. . .for nature gives to
every time and season
some beauties of its own.

Charles Dickens

GOD. . .DOES GREAT THINGS

that we cannot comprehend.

For to the snow he says, "Fall on the earth."

JOB 37:5–6 NRSV

UNTIL ONE FEELS THE SPIRIT OF CHRISTMAS,

there is no Christmas. All else is outward display—
so much tinsel and decorations.
For it isn't the holly, it isn't the snow.
It isn't the tree, not the firelight's glow.
It's the warmth that comes to the hearts of men
when the Christmas spirit returns again.

AUTHOR UNKNOWN

At Christmas, play and make good cheer
For Christmas comes but once a year.

THOMAS TUSSER

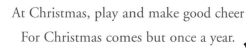

May this holiday season
bring you incomparable joy
and add cheerful memories
too numerous to count.

My best wishes for your merry Christmases and your happy
New Years, your long lives and your true prosperities.

CHARLES DICKENS

BLESSED IS THE SEASON

which engages the whole world
in a conspiracy of love.

HAMILTON WRIGHT MABIE

Christmas evokes so many emotions. . .
fond memories of Christmases past,
pleasure in the present,
hope for the future.

I desire for you a heart filled with peace
and a Christmas that overflows with the Lord's
eternal and rich blessings.

SMILES. *Small kindnesses extended.*
A neighbor bringing a plate of cookies.
A piano playing Christmas carols in a
department store. Cups of wassail
offered in places of business. Clerks and
customers wishing each other Merry Christmas
and Happy Holidays!
Wouldn't it be wonderful if this
thoughtfulness lasted throughout the year?
Maybe it could start with me. . . .

I do come home at Christmas.
We all do, or we all should.
We all come home, or ought to come home, for a
short holiday—the longer, the better—
. . .to take, and give a rest.

CHARLES DICKENS

Christmas is a time for celebration,
a gathering together of family and friends at the
table, amid loads of presents and lavish decoration.
But it's not the food, nor gifts and tinsel—
it's the tenderness of love and care that matters.

What I'd like to have for Christmas
I can tell you in a minute
The family all around me
And the home with laughter in it.

EDGAR A. GUEST

May no gift be too small to give,
nor too simple to receive, which is wrapped in
thoughtfulness, and tied with love.

L. O. BAIRD

i WISH FOR YOU

during this holiday season. . .
family and friends enjoying shared memories
joyous carolers at your door
feet warmed by the hearth
and special moments
of quiet reflection.

COME AND WORSHIP THE REASON

Let the heavens rejoice and the earth be glad before the Lord, for He comes.

From the Offertory of the Christmas Mass, based on Psalm 96:11, 13

FOR UNTO US A CHILD IS BORN,

unto us a son is given:

And the government shall be upon his shoulder:

And his name shall be called

Wonderful, Counsellor, The mighty God,

The everlasting Father, The Prince of Peace.

ISAIAH 9:6 KJV

*I heard the bells on Christmas Day,
their old, familiar carols play, And wild
and sweet the words repeat of peace on
earth, goodwill to men!*

HENRY WADSWORTH LONGFELLOW

And suddenly there was with the angel a multitude
of the heavenly host praising God, and saying,
Glory to God in the highest, and on earth peace,
good will toward men.

LUKE 2:13–14 KJV

*Hark! The herald angels sing,
"Glory to the newborn king!"*

CHARLES WESLEY

Music expresses that which cannot be
put into words and that which cannot remain silent.

VICTOR HUGO

*Music is well said to
be the speech of angels.*

THOMAS CARLYLE

Music, when soft voices die,

Vibrates in the memory.

PERCY BYSSHE SHELLEY

AND THERE WERE. . .

shepherds abiding in the field, keeping watch over their flock by night. And, lo, the angel of the Lord came upon them, and the glory of the Lord shone round about them: and they were sore afraid. And the angel said unto them, Fear not: for, behold, I bring you good tidings of great joy, which shall be to all people. For unto you is born this day in the city of David a Saviour, which is Christ the Lord.

LUKE 2:8–11 KJV

*All this took place to fulfill what the Lord
had said through the prophet: "The virgin will
be with child and will give birth to a son,
and they will call him Immanuel"—
which means, "God with us."*

MATTHEW 1:22–23 NIV

Ever wonder why Jesus wasn't named "Immanuel"?
In Hebrew usage, *"Immanuel"* refers to a characterization—
as in *"God with us"* rather than a title or actual name. It was
God's way of telling us the Messiah would be deity.

But when the fulness of the time was come,

God sent forth his Son.

GALATIANS 4:4 KJV

Joy to the world! The Lord is come,

Let earth receive her King.

ISAAC WATTS

And the Word was made flesh, and dwelt among us,

(and we beheld his glory).

JOHN 1:14 KJV

*Now when Jesus was born in
Bethlehem of Judaea in the days
of Herod the king, behold, there came
wise men from the east to Jerusalem,
saying, Where is he that is born
King of the Jews? For we have seen
his star in the east, and are
come to worship him.*

MATTHEW 2:1–2 KJV

Wonder is the basis of worship.

THOMAS CARLYLE

O come, let us worship
and bow down:
Let us kneel before
the Lord our maker.

PSALM 95:6 KJV

He worships God who knows Him.

SENECA

Take time this Christmastide
to go a little way apart,
And with the help of God prepare
the house that is in your heart.

ANONYMOUS

Celebration is the recognition that something is there and
needs to be made visible so that we can say Yes to it.

HENRI J. M. NOUWEN

*Amid all the festivities
of the season,
don't forget to make room
for Him in your heart.
The Lord wants to spend time
with you—to know you intimately.
Make time for Him, and He will
bless you far beyond anything
you can imagine!*

Christmas won't be Christmas without any presents.

LOUISA MAY ALCOTT, *Little Women*

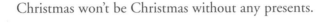

Every good gift and every perfect gift is from above.

JAMES 1:17 KJV

FOR BY GRACE ARE YE SAVED THROUGH FAITH;

and that not of yourselves: it is the gift of God.

EPHESIANS 2:8 KJV

jesus is
the real gift
of Christmas.
♥

Experience the Joy

He put a new song in my mouth,
a hymn of praise to our God.

Psalm 40:3 NIV

ALL OF LIFE IS A GIFT,

and God has given it for joy.

TERRY LINDVALL

And Mary said, My soul doth magnify the Lord,

and my spirit hath rejoiced in God my Saviour.

LUKE 1:46–47 KJV

MAY YOU FIND JOY IN THE MESSIAH'S BIRTH AND EXULT

in a renewed spirit throughout the coming new year.

i WILL HONOR CHRISTMAS iN MY HEART

and try to keep it all the year.

EBENEEZER SCROOGE,
A Christmas Carol by Charles Dickens

Create in me a pure heart, O God,
and renew a steadfast spirit within me.

PSALM 51:10 NIV

AH, FRIENDS, DEAR FRIENDS, AS YEARS GO ON

and heads get gray, how fast the guests do go!
Touch hands, touch hands, with those who stay.
Strong hands to weak, old hands to young, around
the Christmas board, touch hands.
The false forget, the foe forgive, for every guest will
go and the fire burn low
and cabin empty stand.
Forget, forgive, for who may say
that Christmas day may ever come
to host or guest again.
Touch hands!

WILLIAM HENRY HARRISON MURRAY

CELEBRATE THE HAPPINESS

that friends are always giving,
make every day a holiday
and celebrate just living!

AMANDA BRADLEY

*It is easy to forget that each day brings
a new hope, a new experience,
a new sunrise—some small,
gentle reminder that life is
to be appreciated and enjoyed.*

How good is man's life,
the mere living!
how fit to employ;
All the heart and the soul
and the senses
forever in joy!

ROBERT BROWNING

I WISH YOU A CHRISTMAS OVERFLOWING

with the precious gifts that only God gives—
the joy of family. . .
the love of special friends. . .
and the blessing of a refreshed spirit.

May the gift of His Love
be yours this Christmas!